Bitter, Better, Sweeter

Ruzzerh Jake Bacay

Ukiyoto Publishing

All global publishing rights are held by

Ukiyoto Publishing

Published in 2023

Content Copyright © Ruzzerh Jake Bacay

ISBN 9789360169237

All rights reserved.
No part of this publication may be reproduced, transmitted, or stored in a retrieval system, in any form by any means, electronic, mechanical, photocopying, recording or otherwise, without the prior permission of the publisher.

The moral rights of the author have been asserted.

This is a work of fiction. Names, characters, businesses, places, events, locales, and incidents are either the products of the author's imagination or used in a fictitious manner. Any resemblance to actual persons, living or dead, or actual events is purely coincidental.

This book is sold subject to the condition that it shall not by way of trade or otherwise, be lent, resold, hired out or otherwise circulated, without the publisher's prior consent, in any form of binding or cover other than that in which it is published.

www.ukiyoto.com

For my family

Poetry/Prose

"Bitter, Better, Sweeter" is a moving collection of poetry and prose that explores the themes of bitterness, betterment, and sweetness by delving deeply into the author's life. This book gives a fascinating look into the author's distinctive viewpoint on the human journey by drawing on personal experiences and significant life lessons. The writings are observant and cover a wide range of topics, creating a tapestry of feelings and experiences that speak to readers. The author invites readers to join them on a profound and transformational examination of the human spirit through the use of sincere language that conveys the essence of life's trials and successes.

Let the words breathe and spread across the pages

Contents

Part - I	1
Successful Living	3
My Life	4
Part - II	7
Always Smile	9
You told me lie	10
Part - III	13
The Crow's Prey	15
Part - IV	19
In my proper person	20
Keep Trying	23
7:56 PM	24
Part - V	26
My letter for my Papa	28
Part - VI	33
Suffocation	34
Part - VII	40
About the Author	*45*

Part - I

I wish someday a wave will sweep me away and remove me from the place where I am standing. I will let the water touch my body until I can't feel anything anymore or it will drown me completely and take somewhere.

- Ruzzerh Jake Bacay

Successful Living

Success is not about material possessions or fame; it's about being truthful, kind, wise. A person can be successful if they make an effort to avoid lying, swatted scandals, and fought against scandals. Success doesn't require a grand palace, but rather a willingness to make a difference in the world.

-Ruzzerh Jake Bacay

My Life

I hold my life, I will never make my life as miserable as a stray dog,

Because I understand how life is played.

I will never force anyone to believe in me or to be me just to say that I am right they are wrong,

Because I know that the root we come from is different.

And I will never waste all the opportunities that come in my life,

I will wake up every day happy and full of positive outlook and use it as a shield against any problem.

-Ruzzerh Jake Bacay

I saw myself in your eyes: that I was shameful, that I was a big mistake.

Like in every decision and every action, I was wrong.

As if you were saying it with every rustle of my breathe, I was wrong.

Your hug is so gentle, like a cloud, and warm as my morning coffee.

But when I spilled my coffee on my table and hoped that you would swipe it, I was wrong again.

Your delicious embrace became a tight chain; I couldn't break free, and every word of yours hit me in every part of my body.

My sadness had spilled its blood.

Until one word comes out of my mouth, Ma, I will still forgive you as the chain loosens and spreads on the floor.

-Ruzzerh Jake Bacay

"Time is Gold," we often hear that line. When you're young you don't really understand the true meaning of that line because you have a lot of time, time wasted playing online games and watching nonsense videos on the internet, instead of reading a book or to write to enhance your handwriting. But when you get older, you tend to forget a lot, get neglected because of the amount of work. You will understand that line when your life becomes complicated.

-Ruzzerh Jake Bacay

Part - II

Try to use your mind and heart when you make a decision, because it doesn't have a limitation.

-Ruzzerh Jake Bacay

Always Smile

Jokingly expresses happiness and the joy of life. You will receive affection and compliments from others, and you will also receive blessings. Give sincere individuals the task of moaning and weeping because problems are brittle. When facing difficulties, smiling might make things easier. Attempt to chase away whatever sadness you may be feeling.

-Ruzzerh Jake Bacay

You told me lie

You plant a million on your tongue
You shared it with me
I harvest it in my mind

-Ruzzerh Jake Bacay

Don't pity me if you see me as weak. I might just be worn out. I'm sick of trying to reach things that are almost in my line if sight. I'm attempting to tighten my hold, but I'm losing feeling in it. 'Cuz What's the purpose of fighting for your ambition if your motivation to do so is also motivation to give up?

-Ruzzerh Jake Bacay

One day, I asked my mom why I was so different. One of my friends is good at math, and one of my friends is good at art, while I'm not neither good at singing or dancing; I can't even play any instrument. She said that "You are what you are; there is no one else like you. You are more important than anyone else. Don't look at the things they have that you don't have, but pay more attention to how they treat you well because that's what we say you are special.

-Ruzzerh Jake Bacay

Part - III

A relationship is like writing a poem, you will continue to write when you find a beautiful idea and when you start writing and you find it difficult how to make it better or you lose your vocabulary or you can't find the right words to use you will stop and leave it on your table. What you have to do is go over it and do it again.

-Ruzzerh Jake Bacay

The Crow's Prey

I saw a boy too young looking at me, hands on the ground.

bow his hopeless head.

He closed his eyes, but his mind was open.

While the sun seemed to sympathize with him

A crow swooped over his shoulder and grabbed his neck.

The sound of crushed bones as he struggles to break free from a tight stranglehold

His tears shouted and vibrated through his body.

He said, "Don't do this to me, Pa.

-Ruzzerh Jake Bacay

At a family gathering, sometimes it is usually or okay to for our relatives to say the things that they didn't want. Sometimes there is a scolding, instead of the good things that they shared. But even so, the family is the family, it is like a word or a language which has evolved over time but we never forget the origin of it.

-Ruzzerh Jake Bacay

Every syllable that leaves your mouth travels to your razor-sharped teeth

You are a man with a shark's mouth

It hurts when you bite me

-Ruzzeh Jake Bacay

Life is about taking different paths. There are a lot of things that we will face in our journey that we get surprised about or we didn't expect whether it is good or bad. But it is our responsibility to try and adjust to it. The small things that happened in our lives hit differently, it's magical. At times, it is more significant and beautiful if we notice it.

-Ruzzerh Jake Bacay

Part - IV

In my proper person

I'm starting to feel it in me

As my thoughts twist and twirl into my cerebrum

It affects my senses

My eyes start to shine like it has a new lens to ponder something that I'm now in a gender crisis

But when my ears begin to hear a whisper that becomes lofty and suddenly turns into garrous

I have covered my ears with my own perspective, principles and confidence

And start to swallow the bitter taste to a better sweet taste of doubts and fear

The scent of their flower of love, care, and support that defuses the air

I smelled and it like a bomb that booms and help me to bloom

And the seed that planted in me

Now I will reap and share the truth with everybody that I am extraordinary

-Ruzzerh Jake Bacay

In the game of love, there are two types of player – the one who cheats and the person who has been betrayed. Which of those two are you, if you are The cheater, remember that the word sorry cannot replace the word trust and if you are the one who was betrayed, don't be a cheater either because you are not the loser because you are the one who truly loved.

-Ruzzerh Jake Bacay

Every person has their own worldview and set of beliefs. When someone says anything that against our convictions, we often choose not to listen to them in order to maintain our position as the correct one. In other cases, we even degrade their moral character and socioeconomic status in order to further our own cause. It's sad to think that we act in that way, but we will always keep in mind that if we have beliefs that are contrary to theirs, we are fools and they are the intelligent one. Anyone who has ability to understand and practice the spirit of empathy is smarter than everyone else.

-Ruzzerh Jake Bacay

Keep Trying

Every night, a solemn thought comes to mind: "Trying the things that I'm not good at" is a testament to one's efforts and dedication. Whether it's punk or a joke, trying is an effort that represents yourself. At the end of life, one's conscience is serene, and I face the cold river with courage and boldness. The one who tried is a blue-ribbon man, and I must work with eager zest and not falter in my plans.

-Ruzzerh Jake Bacay

7:56 PM

When the light hits your face

And my life was gloomy as a cloud

I'm glad

Seeing you smile at me I forgot my core like a kid on an exam

My skin was touched by your hands

Yet I can still hear your voice in my bones

In the field of petals and leaves that was the roadway, you and I was strolled

When our feet make a crunchy sound

It shows the number of steps we take and memories we create

When lovely aroma turns into a foul meal

And the petals shatter into a pieces of glass

I stop

Where are you?

I can't hear you

Where are you?

I can't find you

When you bend me in silence

And now it's clear that I'm the one who lights up your face

You have now vanished

When the street where I stand looks like a liminal space

When the fire becomes smoke, I suffocated

My lungs feel like they're melting

As I struggled to walk through the glass shards on my path

I won't stop; I will force myself to go back to where you saw me

So that when you try to get to back to me, you will experience the road I took to forget you

-Ruzzerh Jake Bacay

Part - V

Sometime when you are out of your emotions, and a lot of things are going through your mind, and the words that you decided to whisper into your tongue because you were afraid to tell them, but when your heart makes a signal to your brain to speak, your tears always come first.

-Ruzzerh Jake Bacay

My letter for my Papa

My dearest Papa,

How are you?

I miss you

Maybe you still remember when I told you what my dream was. I was said I want to be a fashion designer, but you said no because I should be practical. What if people don't like my work? I said I want to be a teacher, and you said yes, you will support me. But I thought you would see me for what I really wanted to be, but not anymore. There are so any things I wish to share with you, all the things I've dreamt of and hoped for, but the time seemed to escape us before I could express them all.

First, I want to tell you how much I miss you. Your presence was like a warm embrace that made me feel safe and loved, and I long for those moments of laughter and joy we shared together. Your departure left an empty space in my heart, but I want you to know that your love and teachings continue to guide me through life. I wish you could have seen me grow, Pa. I wish you see how I almost reached Mama's height. I've become a good student, just like you always wanted me to be, and I've made friends who support and care for me as you did what exactly is my gender.

I wish you could see my diploma and it says that I have graduated from high school. There are countless milestone I've reached that I wish you were there to witness. I got my first job – a simple planting and pruning – and I felt so proud to earn my own money, just like you thought me about responsibility.

Oh, I wish you could see my beard and mustache. And you hear how people say that I look exactly like you. I wish you could see how I set foot in college. Pa, I wish I could have given you more hugs and told you "I love you" a thousand times more. But I believe you know, even from afar, that you are always in my heart. I want you to know that everything I do is in honor of you, and I hope to make you proud. Thank you for being the best dad a child could ever wish for.

With all my love, Your son

-Ruzzerh Jake Bacay

When you think that you are complete and you feel that the cup of your life is full, you may yet feel as though something is lacking or off but you are unable to identify what it is. Here's the thing: when the cup is full it spills. That's why, while something is added, something is subtracted.

-Ruzzerh Jake Bacay

Three teachings that are woven into our lives:

Accepting changes will bring us growth

Love ferociously because bonds provide more meaning in our lives

Seek information to secure our future

-Ruzzerh Jake Bacay

I never blame you if you can't accept me as part of you or if you can't even give me a single droplet of your love. Because at first, one thing I'm sure I lost was that I was the one who fell first.

-Ruzzerh Jake Bacay

Part - VI

Suffocation

It's delightful to wake up and breathe in a world where you have nothing to prove and you don't have to beg for respect.

-Ruzzerh Jake Bacay

It's okay to get angry and hold a grudge against other people; you have feelings, and that's normal. When you plant, take the time to nurture it, water it with understanding, touch it with joy and a positive outlook, and you will be surprised at the results.

-Ruzzerh Jake Bacay

While you are young; dream as many as you can so that when you get old you can say to yourself that you reach one of them.

-Ruzzerh Jake Bacay

Even while losing a parent, especially when you are young, is painful, nothing compares to the sorrow of witnessing a mother sobbing for her kid.

-Ruzzerh Jake Bacay

I wish my ears could hear your heartbeat and know how load it is and if I'm the reason for it. I want to go into an empty room and listen to how it travels as a sound and turns into merely an echo, and how it's gone.

-Ruzzerh Jake Bacay

I wake up and opens my eyes, aided by yellow mayflowers

A blind-cord drawls across the windowsill,

and I wonder about the conversation and the contents of the jug.

The nurse appears distant, and music and roses burn through crimson slaughter.

I feel cold and hot, with no light to see the voices and no time to dream or ask.

-Ruzzerh Jake Bacay

Part - VII

Sometimes the only way to be happy is to be lonely.

Enjoying the foggy night under the yellow moon and the blanket of cold air.

-Ruzzerh Jake Bacay

We often experience emotional distress and turn to darkness in a happy family. We witness our friends' happiness and think of departed loved ones. We experience melancholy and unusual emotions as a result of this transformation. We can still make out the familiar shapes from long ago, but the ominous silence nudges us with memories of days gone by and passing whimsies.

-Ruzzeh Jake Bacay

The moon look placed and vigilant on a calm night, making it the deal night for dancing. I hooked an ancient white mare to sleigh and harnessed her, letting her enjoy the moonlight ride. The moon's light shed as the old horse and zephyrs raced over the night. The gathering was in awe of the moon's brilliance as the evening was filled with music and poetry.

-Ruzzerh Jake Bacay

The lesson you collect will hold you tight.
A wisdom will whisper in you in your silent flight.

-Ruzzerh Jake Bacay

About the Author

Ruzzerh Jake Bacay is a 20-year-old writer who pulls inspiration from his experiences, the nature of the planet, and human condition. He was raised in Barangay Bubog, San Jose, Occidental Mindoro, a tiny seaside community in the Philippines.

Additionally, Ruzzerh attends Occidental Mindoro State University to pursue a Bachelor of Science in Development Communication.

He works to use his platform to spread awareness of current issues, foster empathy, and advance the idea that the tales we tell have the potential to change the world.

www.ingramcontent.com/pod-product-compliance
Lightning Source LLC
LaVergne TN
LVHW041555070526
838199LV00046B/1978